THE CLASS FROM THE
BLACK LAGOON

STORY BY
MIKE THALER

PICTURES BY
JARED LEE

Cartwheel
·B·O·O·K·S·®

SCHOLASTIC INC.

New York   Toronto   London   Auckland   Sydney
Mexico City   New Delhi   Hong Kong   Buenos Aires

To kids in every grade, you are all very special
—M.T.

To my wife P.J.,
who's in a class all by herself
—J.L.

ISBN-13: 978-0-545-08544-1
ISBN-10: 0-545-08544-6

Text copyright © 2002 by Mike Thaler.
Illustrations copyright © 2002 by Jared D. Lee Studio, Inc.

10 9 8   40   12 13/0
Printed in the U.S.A. · This edition first printing, September 2008

It's the first day of school, and I have a new class coming in one hour. I heard they're *really* weird and that they put their last three teachers into early retirement.

I also heard that when the class gets to school, they all turn into horrible ghouls! And they emit odd odors and make strange sounds.

Some grow two noses so they can pick them at the same time.
They love *scratch* and *sniff*.

I heard that some have orange hair, some have green hair, some have purple hair, and some have *no hair*!

They're great at making horrible faces. They can roll their eyeballs back into their heads so only the whites are showing.

And some can cover both their noses with their lips and wiggle their ears.

They can wrap their bodies in and around their chairs so tightly that sometimes they have to be pried off with crowbars.

One teacher said they tie themselves to their desks with their shoelaces.
I guess it's a safety precaution.

I heard they eat crayons, chalk, and erasers. They drink ink, chew pencils, love to mumble, and tear paper into tiny little bits.

They also make spitballs the size of cannonballs.
But the thing they're best at making…is noise!

They're all virtuosos with Velcro,
and drummers with pencils.

Every part of their bodies is a musical instrument.
Put it all together and you have a symphony orchestra.

Their other area of expertise is *excuses*.

"We were late because the school bus was attacked by pirates."

And they're *always* late when they come to school.
But they only come when they have highly contagious diseases.

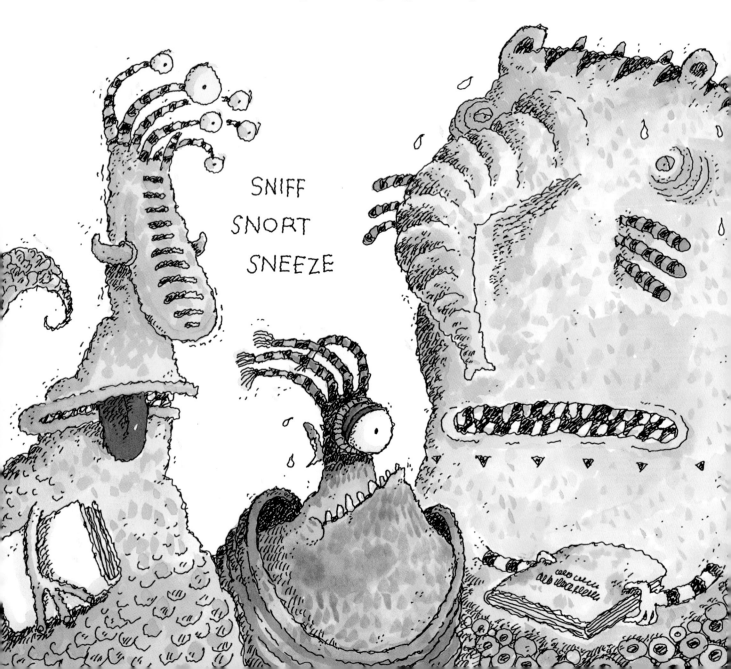

SNIFF
SNORT
SNEEZE

Instead of dotting their *i*'s and crossing their *t*'s, they cross their *eyes* and dot their *teeth*.

When they're *healthy*,
they stay home.

In class, they're always waving their hands in the air
to go to the bathroom or to give silly answers like,
"What's George Washington's last name?"
"Bridge!"

They do love to write. They
on the walls, and they write
they don't write on... is their papers.

There are other things about school they love:
pestering teachers, poking peers, and using the
electric pencil sharpener. They call it Mr. Shred.

And he runs all day because they break their points on purpose just to use him, over and over and over again. At the end of the day, I'll be standing waist-deep in pencil shavings.

Oh, my, it's almost 8 o'clock! I'd better check
my survival kit: helmet, hockey pads, earplugs.
Well, I guess I'm ready.

Wow! They're all cheery and clean,
and each one has only one nose.

"Here's an apple and some flowers, Mrs. Green."
"Well, thank you, class."

The flowers were picked from the front of the school, and the apple had sixteen bites out of it. But, hey, no one's perfect. It's the thought that counts.

I'm going to love this class.